# TOWN OF SHADOWS

# TOWN OF SHADOWS

LINDSAY STERN

Scrambler Books 2012
Sacramento, CA

**Town of Shadows**
@2012 Lindsay Stern

Published by Scrambler Books
www.scramblerbooks.com
Sacramento, California
Fiction series no.3
Cover art and design by Kady Dennell

1st Paperback edition
ISBN: 978-0-578-11259-6
Printed in the USA

# ACKNOWLEDGEMENTS

This book is dedicated to my parents, Glynnis O'Connor and Douglas Stern, and my sister, Hana Stern, to whom I owe everything, including the unflagging encouragement and wisdom that made it possible.

Thank you to my extended family, particularly to my grandmothers, Lenka Peterson and Ruby Stern, for their love of questions, and to Brian O'Connor and Rick Stern for their conversation, to which these pages owe a great deal.

Thank you to my teachers and professors, especially Alexander George, Daniel Hall, Jee Leong Koh, Joseph Reiser and Helaine Smith, who have taught me how and why to think.

Thank you to Laura Goode, Paul Griffin, Thomas Hummel, Patricia Morrisroe and Andrew Zolot for their incalculable support and editorial acuity.

Thank you to the constellation of friends whose humor and insight have enabled this book and my sanity.

Thank you to Kai Goldynia, whose sense of wonder, curiosity and understanding have enlightened me.

Thank you, finally, to the three people whose brilliance and humanity have taught me the difference between cave and sun (cf. *The Republic*, 514a-521d): Susan Sagor, Adam Sitze, and eternally, as ever, Laura Mahr.

*for my family*

# CONTENTS

# THE WHITE BALLOON, PART I

How the world happened, according to Pierre:

## I

In the beginning, the Child
took her hourglass by the throat,
rolled it forth and back till the sand spun.

## II

On the walls of her room the Child
drew wind, and on the ceiling the Child drew stars.

## III

And the Child took her mother
apart, limb by limb, and found
a rib where her voice had been.
And the Child took her father
apart, bone by bone, and found
a clot of dust behind his eyes.

## IV

Soon the Child found
that the room was dust, too,
and bone, and that the sand
in the glass was still spinning.

## V

So the Child left the room.
And outside there was nothing
to spin, or to take apart—nothing
to roll, nothing to draw, nothing to leave.

## VI

Outside the Child found a white balloon.
And the Child bit a hole in the balloon,
and whispered her name.
She tied a knot, lifted her eyes, and let it go.

# ARITHMETIC

The town schoolhouse was built of sleet. From several angles it appeared two-dimensional, an iron mass propped against the horizon. Inside, the teacher was writing problems on the board:

$$\text{sound} + \text{sound} =$$

$$\text{clock} - \text{hands} =$$

$$\text{today} / \text{day} =$$

She turned to the class. Dozens of eyes peered back, unblinking.

"Terrence!" she barked.

A boy peeled himself from his chair and shuffled forward. He stood trembling as she handed him the chalk.

$$\text{sound} + \text{sound} = \textit{sound}$$

"Correct."

The room exhaled. Terrence set the chalk against the board once more, sliding his tongue to one corner of his lips.

clock – hands = *pulse*

Again, the teacher nodded. Her lids were no farther than an inch from her bangs, and flickered on and off as he wrote.

today / day = *zero*

The air grew still.

"Alice," the teacher called, "correct him."

A tall, bluish girl advanced to the board. Deftly she slid the chalk from Terrence's fist.

today / day = ~~*zero*~~ *now*

The teacher smiled, parted her lips. But Alice was writing again, more quickly:

*thinking / thought*

She continued:

$$= \mathcal{I}$$

The teacher's brows vanished behind her hair.

"Incorrect," she announced, "Alice's terms are invalid. Intelligent children do not think. They solve."

# HIS AUTOBIOGRAPHY

Pierre keeps it under the sink. It reads:

<u>Pierre</u>
*January*: Birth.
*February*: Childhood.
*March*: Pierre is a boy of ambitions.
*April*: Pierre makes his living extracting salt from
seawater.
*May*: Pierre marries Selma.
*June*: Pierre and Selma buy a house with daffodil
wallpaper.
*July*: A chandelier falls on Pierre.
*August*: Pierre recovers.
*September*: Pierre learns to play the flute.
*October*: For Halloween, Pierre is a frayed hem.
*November*: [unwritten]
*December*: Pierre becomes a rug doctor.

# SELMA

Selma has not read his autobiography. Neither has Pierre; he knows the plot.

Selma is a novelist. She communicates through blinking. In November, she wrote a book about a town in which nobody died. Pierre disliked the story. He thought it absurd, and told her so. Selma was furious. She spat on him. So Pierre apologized: "My words are like toothpaste, Selma, easy to emit but difficult to retract."

"You are an idiot," Selma blinked.

# THE MAYOR

For a long time the mayor required all citizens to wear small wooden cages on their heads. The idea was to trap their thoughts before they wafted behind another's eyes, between another's ears. At first the results were satisfactory. Then came the complications: the cages filled until the mayor could no longer distinguish one face from the next. Through the bars he discerned only light— red for politicians, for philosophers bright blue, and for children the glint of candleflame. They were happily blind, watching their thoughts unfold before them as the objects of the world ticked on.

Soon the mayor tired of the cages. Bureaucrats sawed off the bars until the ground was laced with splintered wood.

"It's for the best," said the mayor through his black cigar.

They watched the ash descend into his empty sleeves. They watched him with one face.

# CONSTELLATIONS

Pierre stores his tools in a bassinet. On the pillow is a family of needles. Pierre owns a needle of every size. Last night, he found constellations of rips in the rug. Rips are not unusual, so Pierre is constantly on his knees. Sometimes he leaves a needle on the floor. Selma does not appreciate this. No matter, he thinks. There is nothing worse than a wounded carpet.

# THE NOISE

George was an ordinary boy in an ordinary house, on a day like any other. He swung his heels out of bed, swallowed his breakfast, and arrived at school on time. The blackboard, as usual, was white with word equations.

As he set to work on the first equation, George discovered a new corridor in his mind. At the end of the corridor was a door, and inside was a noise he recognized. The noise was too large for the room. It spilled into the corridor. Hastily George shut the door, but the noise seeped around the hinges. The noise was the color of rain.

Only then did George notice the other doors. They lined the corridor like eyelids, like rows upon rows of closed eyes. All of the doors were seeping.

George turned and began walking briskly. He tried to find his way back to the blackboard, to the windows and chalk and equations. But the corridor stretched on, without entrance.

# THE LEXICON

Lately, Pierre has felt his brain expanding. Growing lighter, as if swollen with air. This morning, a thrust against the roof of his skull. Last night, a pressure in his jaw. Before long, he suspects, the whole machine will burst. Words will trickle through his ears, scamper back into the world. So as not to forget them, he has built a lexicon:

Mirror, n. A palindrome.

Loneliness, n. Wordlessness.

Indigestion, n. Swallowed noise.

[cont.]

# THE CHIMNEYSWEEP

Victor had dissected every home in town. He came and left unnoticed, slinking down each house's spine. From there he heard the sounds of other organs—the slosh of bathwater, the clicking stove, the fluttering of pages upstairs. Mother reading, Victor guessed. Those horizontal lives.

Victor avoided live chimneys. Even the coldest left him black. One night a child asked him if he was made of smoke.

"Why yes," he said. "I've spent the day arranging flames."

That night, Victor had dissected an empty house. He'd hung above the sleeping coal, counting the sighs of contracting wood. When he'd climbed back into the night above, the house was still breathing.

# THE BANKER

Eleven stories above the town, in the offices of Platterstain & Co., Harold discovered in his left heel an insatiable itch. Beside him the other bankers tapped and clicked and murmured, scribbling numbers, loosening ties. The daily briefing would begin in a moment. Harold rose from his chair with the others, shuffling toward the table in the center of the room. Florescent bulbs chilled the air, the cufflinks, the bald scalps. The bankers were seated now, adjusting their suits. Their eyes were the windows of one vacant house.

As the briefing commenced, Harold's itch grew worse. He slipped his foot from his shoe and dragged his heel along the edge of the table leg. From the corner of his eye he watched the banker beside him. She hadn't noticed. She was blackening her notepad with a string of numbers, obscuring each sum with the next.

Harold realized with horror that the itch was spreading. It clawed across the sole of his foot, and around his toes. Soon his entire foot was roaring. He peeked under the table, slipping off the remains of his sock. Except for the twitching, his foot appeared unchanged. Desperately he dragged his sole across the carpet, colliding with the blade of a high heel. The banker beside him jerked. She swung her chin in his direction, and he saw that her entire face was blank. The itch had caked his vision, frozen his tongue. He tried to laugh, but the smile dangled from his jaw, then dropped. It lay on the floor like a stunned worm.

"If you'll excuse me," he mumbled, stumbling from the table.

A dozen more chins swung toward him, a dozen faces blank as plates. Harold limped down the hall, toward the Currency Room. The itch had climbed to his knee. All he heard was the roaring of his foot, louder now, the syllables of some tremendous, undreamt sum.

## EXPERIMENT 1: HOW TO FREEZE

Before marrying Selma, Pierre composed a series
of experiments. Experiment 1 reads:

### Materials:

Thimble, snow, water, bowl.

### Procedure:

1.  Fill bowl with water.

2.  Breathe onto surface of water.

3.  After ripples escape, add
    thimbleful of silence.

4.  Let steep.

5.  Place bowl in snow.

6.  Wait.

7.  When water clots, smack bowl
    with fist.

8.  Watch ice bloom in fissures.

9.  Remove bowl from snow.

10. Shatter bowl.

Icicle, n. A brief spear.

# THE EVAPORATION OF WORDS

Every third month, the bureaucrats emptied the library. They carted books out by the dozens, spreading them open across the town green, for the sun to drink. Gradually the chapters would fade, line by line, until all that remained were the dots on the i's. When those vanished, the bureaucrats would cart the books back onto the shelves.

# THE MIRROR

Felix was knotting his tie when he noticed that he'd left himself in the mirror. He checked his watch: forty past. He'd be late for work, without question. Anxiously he paced the glass from end to end, thrusting his palms against the wooden frame. Nothing budged. He swung his head into the glass, but cracked his vision instead, collapsing beneath a swarm of yellow gnats. When they dimmed, he examined his room. Nothing seemed to have changed. His sheets lay wrinkled, his shoes untied. By the window his coffee still steamed.

Felix considered. The best way out is the way in, he thought. In his mind he retraced the morning, miming every gesture, every frown. He paid special attention to the memory of the tie. Standing before the mirror, he had looped it round his neck. As he knotted, he had noticed something curious: his pupils were dilating at great speed, consuming his irises and the surrounding whites. Soon they had let in so much light that he could hardly see. It must have happened then, Felix thought, when the bedroom vanished. A flash of light and I became my reflection. Nothing to do now but wait.

Only then did Felix realize that he was not alone. Something brushed against his shoulders, caught the end of his tie. He wheeled around. A man was walking away from him, deeper into the glass. Felix caught the scent of a familiar cologne. He called out, but the man did not turn. Warily Felix set out after him. He was inches away when he felt around his ankles a pair of tiny hands. He started, nearly crushing the figure below. Blinking up at him was an infant, a boy with almond eyes and a single tooth.

"Hello there," said Felix. "Have we met?"

The infant frowned. He was studying the glass beside Felix.

"Aye!" said the infant, "Eye, I!"

The air thickened. On his neck Felix discerned a new warmth. He turned to find a stranger before him, a young man with almond eyes and a mouthful of teeth. The man was looking past him, but Felix did not notice. His mind had drained. Every thought had bled through the sieve of his brain, around his lungs, along his arms, out his fingertips. The thoughts piled on the ground, intact, like bulb upon bulb of mercury.

The young man was Felix. Around his neck was a tie Felix had lost long ago, on his finger a bronze wedding ring. He was looking beyond the mirror, into the bedroom. Felix followed his gaze.

The room was filled with mourners. They moved from wall to wall, murmuring, sipping glasses of Scotch. Felix watched them dwindle and depart, nodding gravely, still sipping. One woman remained. She closed the door and stood alone. Felix did not allow himself to recognize the woman as his wife.

"Ella," he mouthed, "Ella, please."

It was useless, he knew. He watched her tip her chin back and inhale deeply. A sob loomed in her throat, then dissolved. She smoothed her blouse, ran a palm over her hair. She left the room.

Felix felt his muscles transform into broth. He slid to the ground, breathing in knots. The yellow gnats returned, lancing the weight of her absence, of his. Felix did not smell the lemon of evening tea, nor watch the last guests filter from the lawn. He did not hear, as it loped by, the engine of the now empty hearse.

Self, n. A hidden crowd.

# THE LOGICIAN

For breakfast he ate stewed eggs and a slice of pear. He read the newspaper. He rinsed his plate. He tossed the pear skins in the wastebasket. He read the newspaper again.

The newspaper contained a new edict, signed by the mayor. It read:

> BEYOND ADMINISTRATIVE PURPOSES, THE USE OF VOWELS IS HEREBY FORBIDDEN.

Beside the newspaper were a pen and a sheet of paper. The logician began to write.

> D--r S-r,
> Pl--s- -xpl--n.
> S-nc-r-ly),
> Dr. -

The logician sealed the letter, opened the front door, and counted his steps to the mailbox. The number was always the same. The logician did not notice. He never strayed from the present, even in thought. Memory was dislocation, and no person could occupy two places at once.

The logician counted fifty steps. He did not notice the wind, nor the melting sun. He did not notice the bureaucrat striding across the road, toward the graveyard. The bureaucrat was no taller than a broom. In one hand she held a brush, in the other a jar of black paint. The logician was climbing his front steps as she knelt beside the first grave. She crossed out one vowel, then another. By lunchtime she was finished. The next morning, the gravestones would stand as they always had. The logician would not notice the drops of paint on the road, nor the host of dismembered names.

# BY THE WINDOW

Pierre awoke to find he had lost his shadow. He is still sitting by the window, whistling hymns through two teeth. Beside him are a crinkled slip of paper, a flute, and a little tin cyclist painted red. He is naked. Selma will not notice because she is blind. She is also mute, as she lost her voice cheering in the war. Even so, he can tell she is ashamed of him. He is always losing things.

## EXPERIMENT 2: HOW TO SWIM

### Materials:
Water, hands, feet.

### Procedure:
1. Lift hands to surface.

2. Flap once.

3. Notice water's modesty in feigning monochromatism.

4. Flap twice.

5. Lift mouth to surface.

6. Kick once.

7. Breathe to avoid becoming a thought.

8. Kick twice.

9. Watch: at high temperatures, water may shed.

10. Do not mistake evaporation for flight.

# THE LEPIDOPTERIST

Leopold was a collector of butterflies. Swallow-tails, clearwings, monarchs, whites. He kept them in the pantry. In the evenings, they hung from the drinking straws, asleep, leaving a pulsing sound in their wake. Leopold would run a flashlight over the pantry shelves, across the boxes and jars. Now and then he'd rouse a butterfly, and turn the pantry into a box of wind.

In the schoolhouse, Leopold had learned the Law of Non-Contradiction:

"Opposites cannot occur simultaneously."

Across the blackboard the teacher had chalked the following symbols:

$$\sim(P \wedge \sim P)$$

In his notebook Leopold had written:

$$\sim()\sim$$

That afternoon Leopold had caught his first butterfly, a monarch. He had spent all night on the pantry floor, watching it weave in and out of his flashlight's beam. When it settled on a drinking straw, he was overwhelmed by the desire to weep. Instead, he laughed. He laughed and wept, wept and laughed, until he lost track of which was which.

The next morning, Leopold began to toy with opposites. He plucked the monarch from its drinking straw. On each of its wings, he wrote a word:

*Empty*          *Full*

As the monarch fluttered back into the shelves, he watched the wingwords fuse and clash, clash and fuse. He repeated the experiment with each butterfly he caught:

*Separate*          *Whole*

*Many*          *Few*

*Lonely*          *Loved*

By fall, he would open the pantry door to find a blizzard of words and wings.

Flight, n. The dance of antonyms.

# THE PLAGUE OF DREAMS

Within a week, half the town had contracted the dream. It was highly contagious. Quarantine signs sprang up like dandelions.

"Plagues strike for a reason," said the mayor. He was miles away. His voice came from the mouth of an enormous gramophone. Flecks of ash descended from its lips. The bureaucrats held the gramophone as they would a vase of endangered birds.

"That's right," a girl whispered. "It was aiming for you."

One of the bureaucrats heard the girl. He had her deleted.

In the dream, the sleeper encountered a wooden box. The box was full of Nothing. The townspeople knew no words with which to express the dream, because words were nothing without things, which were nothing without words. The Nothing hung between words and things like a mirror.

Once a person saw the Nothing, she became it. Suddenly there was nothing to do, nothing to say, nothing to be. Nothings roamed the town like silent noise.

The deleted girl had not been infected. She had woken the previous night to find her father clutching the air.

# THE LOST YEAR

Weeks later, the plague emerged in a different form. It swept the town into a thick sleep. For twelve months it climbed through the drawers of each mind, sorting, rearranging, and leaving everyone, at last, as he had been. The next morning, no one realized he had slept for more than a night. The seasons had spun without residue. What little evidence there was escaped attention—soft tires, skins of dust on windowsills. Lamps left on had sputtered out, but still the sun roared. No one remembered his dreams.

## THE PHYSICIST

Shortly after the second plague, the physicist was deleted for violating Newton's laws. The bureaucrats found her on the town green, converting objects into light. She would toss a stone into the air, watch it climb and vanish. On the evening of her death, it rained in color.

# THE TREE NURSERY

Arabella was a breeder of shapes. Triangles, mostly. Evergreens with cylindrical spines. On their fingers she draped tassels and rings, beads and tinsel threads, until the trees became their own source of light.

Arabella was a braider of wreaths. Gently she sheared the down from each branch, bound the bristles into tongues of green, and looped them round a hanger. The hangers were transparent. Most slept along the banister, or on the bathtub's lip. Arabella strung the rest with twine, and hung them from the mouth of the chimney. In storms they splayed around the roof like hair. Some broke free and soared away, over the hills. Others hid among the trees, waiting for mice.

Spring had fallen when Arabella discovered the boy. He was sleeping under an evergreen, in a nest of dropped tassels. Tinsel dangled from the boughs, windless, like drop upon drop of stunned rain.

The boy learned quickly. He sheared and braided, looped and bound. Despite the cold, he refused to come inside. He ate nothing but leaves, and drank water only after it had collected light.

Arabella would hand him his water glass, and watch as he held it to the sun. On cloudy days she brought him a match.

When a dozen wreaths were finished, Arabella and the boy set out for the graveyard. The boy wore a crown of hangers. Strands of beads trailed behind them, tracing their course. When they arrived, they draped the wreaths across each soldier's stone. Around them mourners knelt beside the graves, chuckling, scolding, tracing the names that only they remembered. All morning they held conversations with the dead, passing each other without a glance. Today Arabella knelt too, laying her hand on one woman's arm.

"He's quite old, now, you know," she murmured.

The woman looked toward Arabella as she would an object on the horizon.

"Why no," she said, "He's just collecting time."

To love, v. To live twice.

# IN THE PARLOR

Pierre is a collector of trinkets. In the parlor are rows of metal figures and a china cat. Pierre has composed a flute sonata for each. Before playing, he arranges his audience on the windowsill. He hopes his music sounds like a child clearing her throat. Today he will perform for the cyclist: Adagio in D.

# THE POET

Lita knew from age twelve that no person was entirely human. Most were several degrees off, while others were unrecognizable. Lita's mother, for instance, was down to 94%. She had lost 1% in childbirth, and 5% on an afternoon in May, when she returned from an errand to find her swimming pool filled with drowned hens. From the morning she wrote her first line, Lita knew that poets were not human at all, but a breed of arachnid.

The first line Lita wrote was the following:

1 *VERB VERB VERB PRONOUN VERB VERB VERB*

The possibilities were limitless:

2 *TO DROWN IS TO BREATHE WHAT SHOULD BE SWALLOWED.*

3 *TO LIVE IS TO KNOW WHAT CANNOT BE SAVED.*

Lita preferred line 1, in which the pronoun was a mirror. In lines 2 and 3 the words weren't words anymore, but the limbs of sentences. She liked them well enough, for their meaning. But in meaning their symmetry was lost.

Outside of poems, Lita didn't care for words. The schoolhouse had taught her only that the things worth learning were impossible to teach. Lita knew that the things worth learning lived in pens, and typewriters. The things worth learning were allergic to chalk.

Before the morning of lines 1, 2 and 3, Lita had other ideas. A poet was not an arachnid, she had thought, but an engineer. A poet's job was to build a real human, 100%. 100% humans were only possible on a page. For months Lita wrote, only to find that her characters were reflections of herself. Lita's percentage was approaching zero. Her best characters were at least 90% short.

Lita hit zero on the morning of lines 1, 2 and 3, the day after the drowning of the hens. She had returned home to find her mother face down, flapping across the pool. On her back were three limp hens. The rest were underwater, drifting down like grenades. Now and then Lita's mother would suck a mouthful of air, her swollen face bright against the blue. Mother looks exactly like a hen, Lita thought. It was her first simile.

The rest came easily. Metaphors, too, slipping from her mind into her pen. They were invisible threads, Lita knew, tying one object to the next— dew to tears, sand to time, parents to poultry. She smiled at the memory of her younger poems, at each flawed version of herself. A good poem, she thought, contained no humans at all. A good line was the strand of a web.

When her mother emerged from the pool, caked in feathers, Lita could see that the 5% was irretrievable. She helped dispose of the casualties, and towel-dried one stammering survivor. On her mother's desk she left line 3.

# EXPERIMENT 3: HOW TO WRITE

Materials:

Bird, page, acorn, ink.


Procedure:

1.  Fill acorn cap with ink.

2.  Find sleeping bird.

3.  Slide quills from bird.

4.  Watch follicles wink.

5.  Dip first quill in acorn cap.

6.  Wait.

7.  Watch first word appear, clothe itself in ink.

8.  Repeat steps 5-7 until all quills are black.

9.  Wrap bird in page.

10. Unbloom.

## EYELASHES

Clarence awoke to find his lashes tangled. He lay
for several minutes behind closed lids, listening to
the noise of breakfast. Brows trembling, he tried
once more to pry his lids apart. At last he
discerned a thread of light beyond the black
netting, and his pupils gaped hungrily. The light
was no wider than a hangnail, but to Clarence it
looked like dawn. Beyond his window the sun was
just clearing the church steeple, bleeding color like
a runny yolk. Unoriginal, thought Clarence, both
the simile and the sun itself—plunging up and
down for no reason. He decided to invent a
second sun, on his own black canvas, that would
survey the town with something more than
indifference. Smiling into his quilt, he suspected he
was better off this way, released into a world of
partial darkness, blind to all that he knew.

Happiness, n. Selective sight.

# THE HOROLOGIST

Jerome kept his patients in rows. Across the bookshelves, against the sink, balanced lengthwise along the banister. They ticked so loudly that Jerome had forgotten the sound of his own heartbeat. Even his organs throbbed in time with his patients, with their collective pulse. Jerome enjoyed their company. He would slip out of bed, fix his tea, and spend the morning at the window. When there was no one to cure, he watched for new patients, flipping his shutters open and closed until his house appeared to be blinking.

Jerome's patients were clocks. Wall clocks, watches, even sundials. Their infections were temporary, and often mild. He could trace most afflictions to a chink in the ratchet, a missing pin, or a clotted notch in the minute wheel. In almost all cases, recovery was swift. Sometimes Jerome installed a second, barely visible infection, to ensure the possibility of return.

Jerome would be buried in a clock. A grandfather clock, whose pendulum stood bronze and limbless in the hall closet. Beside it were the shards of an old experiment: a wind-up calendar, its pages scattered now among spools of wire. The pages were labeled by month, the days by number.

Jerome had glued the pages to a wooden spool, which he nailed to a length of branch. He used the branch as a lever, setting the spool in a cradle and winding the calendar round and round until its pages resembled wings. Year acceleration, he called it. The seasons had spun from autumn to spring so quickly that the blood in his thermometer splashed up and down, leaving a ruby film on the glass.

One morning a girl had come knocking, carrying a brightly colored watch. Jerome had held the watch to his ear and listened for a pulse. Next, he'd examined the face. The minute hand was crawling at an hour's pace, while the second hand had stopped altogether.

"Nothing serious," said Jerome. Still, the girl said nothing. She watched Jerome unscrew the metal lid and dip his tweezers into the joints of the machine. Within moments the hands were awake, clicking along at their natural pace.

"Cured," Jerome pronounced. The girl was watching him still, her face a question.

"Do you know the secret of time?" she asked.

Jerome sighed. "The secret of time is that it isn't," he said. "It's your invention, see, and you can measure it as you please. If you chose to live by milliseconds, the world would transform—or rather, you would see things as they always were, at a different speed. A minute would dilate into hours. Bullets would crawl, and birds would appear to be flying in place."

The girl frowned. "And if I lived by years?"

"Ah, if you lived by years—each month a second, say—the world would be unrecognizable. You'd find your hair spilling from your scalp, and the sky ablaze. Cliffs would liquefy into sand."

The girl opened her mouth, then closed it.

"Like I said, you can live at any speed you like. Reality is a question of pace. Let me know, and I'll fix your watch accordingly."

"Well, what do you live by?" the girl said finally. "Seconds, hours?" She glanced at Jerome's watch, whose face lay strapped against his wrist.

Jerome smiled. "I've a tempo all my own."

Time, n. The illusion of change.

# THE DELETION OF ARTISTS

Only several townspeople could recall the deletion of artists. Most replaced the memory with another. The evidence lay about the town, untouched— shredded wreaths, buried clocks, dismembered poems. Within days, the shards were more familiar than earth.

# EXPERIMENT 4: HOW TO FORGET

## Materials:

Light bulb, magnet, drill.

## Procedure:

1. Drill hole in bulb.

2. Locate memory.

3. With magnet, extract memory from eyes.

4. Trap memory in hands.

5. Notice the melody of wings on skin.

6. Lift memory to bulb.

7. Open hands.

8. Watch memory flutter through hole, to filament.

9. Turn bulb on.

10. Notice the flames.

# THE GLOBE

Every morning at dawn, Elijah knelt beside his globe. He saw the continents as the features of a second face, an ally to watch him as he slept. The oceans were yellow with age, the poles dusty. Indonesia was peeling. Japan was half-demolished, its yellow peaks wafting to the rug. With his thumb Elijah traced the remains of France. Paris had melded with *Évreux*, *Fréjus* with Cannes. Every city in Europe had fused with its neighbor, smudges wrought by years of fingerplay. Decay was inevitable, Elijah knew. His globe was no less mortal than his skull.

Inside Elijah's globe was a colony of ants. Months ago a pair had entered through a gap in the equator, a crack just below Guatemala. Since then they'd multiplied beyond count. Elijah watched them trundle along the seam of the world, shouldering crumbs like beige moons. Little Atlases, he thought. He pictured them inside, piled at the south pole, chewing galaxies of toast.

Now and then Elijah left a drop of honey beside the crack, or smeared it across South America. The first time the ants had gone mad with elation, dropping their crumbs into space. They'd rippled across one another, forming an island off the coast of Brazil. Their footsteps had reduced every capital city to a grayish smear.

Before bed, Elijah knelt again beside his globe. He watched the ants make their nightly rounds, and smiled once more at the ruins. Hours later, as he slept, a wasp would mount the globe's wooden stand. With a force no weaker than gravitation, the scent of dried honey would draw it up, past Chile, along the membrane of Peru. The air inside the globe was as black as the ants, and through it the wasp would buzz, beating like a neuron against the cardboard bone, toward one narrowed eye of light.

# THE EQUATION

The next morning in school, Elijah wrote the
following equation on the board:

$$Mind\ /\ Brain = x$$

The teacher blinked. She picked up the telephone.

Within an hour, a bureaucrat had led Elijah away.

Answer, n. A question disguised.

# THE RAILROAD

Doris woke, as usual, beside a cargo train. Plumes of exhaust funneled from her husband's nose, only to vanish again between his lips. His snores rattled the mirror, loosened the dust. He throbbed and shuddered and trembled and heaved. Bleakly Doris surveyed the commotion.

"Wake up, Neville," she said. "I don't love you and I never have."

The train clattered on. Doris decided, as she often did, that she would prefer a plant.

Breakfast hour. Doris slipped down the corridor to the kitchen. Wisps of steam curled from the dishwasher, glazing the counter and frosting the sink. When Doris released the latch, the whole room swam with mist. Inside, clean mugs dripped like molars. Doris pulled tooth after tooth, wiping the glasses dry and dropping fistfuls of spoons into the utensil drawer. The spoons were pins. The drawer was Neville's pillowcase.

Doris noticed that the train had paused. New silence wafted down the corridor, dissolved the kitchen steam. A sigh, the sound of trousers.

Neville standing like a wrench in the corridor's throat.

Doris smiled. Their marriage was a painting of which she was the gloss. Neville supplied the image—the reds and yellows, the crests of paint. The landscape was unremarkable, and crudely drawn. One day, Doris thought, she would scrap the canvas. Leave it naked on Main Street for the trolley wheels to shred.

"Good morning, dear!" she called.

## EXPERIMENT 5: HOW TO SEE

Materials:

Camera, bell jar, moth.


Procedure:

1.  Set camera to ten-minute exposure.

2.  Find a sleeping moth.

3.  Place bell jar over moth.

4.  Wait.

5.  Watch the lens swallowing light.

6.  Notice the chest-clock throb, quicken.

7.  Wait.

8.  Notice the chest-clock slow, sputter out.

9.  Watch the shutter blink.

10. Notice the wings.

Photograph, n. A stunned pulse.

# THE WARD

Born in a white room and he became Eleven. Two followed him down the corridor to the white stairs. Together they chewed on pencils and dreamed of nurse.

"I dreamed, I dream, I will have dreamed," said Eleven.

Two nodded. "You end where you begin."

Soon they'd chewed off the yellow, down to the lead.

Two closed his eyes and wrote a sentence on the wall. Eleven did the same. When they opened their eyes they found that they'd written a poem about an alphabet and an oven and the problem of noise. They watched the poem until its letters broke loose and darted across the walls in fantastic patterns.

Sixteen appeared with a book in his hands. The book read, THE TIN SOLDIER. It was far too loud. Eleven closed his eyes while Two made a circling sound. Sixteen laughed and laughed, pried Eleven's lids apart.

Eleven watched the book. It was red and screaming. Two had circled the DIE in SOLDIER.

They barely noticed nurse. She made a clicking with her tongue. She took the book and led them back into the white.

# THE EXECUTIONER

Blake disliked the deletion room. The wooden throne, the eyeless walls. The listless glow wafting from the lamp. Every evening the room came alive. Blake would lead his charge to the door, lace him with wire, and wait in the clenched air while the victim's body sang. Occasionally Blake would give him something to bite—a pencil, his left sock. As the room thickened with noise he would close both eyes, erasing sensation with thought.

Last night Blake had deleted Seventeen, an ambassador who spoke in palindromes. The night before he had deleted Three, a young poet who refused to drain the vowels from her verse. That deletion had been especially sour. Blake had crushed his lids together, scouring his mind for distraction. He settled on a newspaper article he'd read the week before, about a ringmaster fired for beating clowns.

This evening's deletion was Nine, an attorney with pale, ringless hands. He was impeccably groomed, his nails bright as electric bulbs. Each morning, he shaved every inch of his skin, including his wrists and nose. Tonight Blake approached to find him shaving his forehead.

"It's time," Blake said, addressing the floor.

Nine only hummed.

Blake exhaled. "You seem to like it here more than I do."

Nine considered, razor poised. "One could say so."

"Ever wish you could get out?"

"Often."

Nine had moved on to his lashes, dragging the razor over the half-moons of his lids. "I wouldn't be here at all if it weren't for a troubling habit I have."

"Habit?"

"Yes. Of switching people off."

"What do you mean?"

"Oh, I won't bore you with details." He was shaving the edge of his eyelid now. "It's as simple as it sounds. I've had it since childhood—I used to walk through the garden at night and switch off the insects, one by one, with a butter knife. Later I moved on to rodents, until one day I found a child scuttling through my lawn and switched her off."

Blake held his eyes on the blade. He found himself thinking again of the ringmaster. The man's photograph was printed on the second page, taken outside the courthouse after the verdict was announced. He was a short, ordinary-looking fellow, his face all undone.

"Then came the difficulties," Nine sighed. Blood was threading down his cheek, but he didn't seem to notice. "Well, I'm just about done!"

Blake held out his hand. "I'll take the razor, sir."

"What's that?"

"I'll take the razor."

"Steady now," said the man. A smile crept across his face and continued past his jaw, around his neck.

Like a noose, Blake thought, that smile. He watched Nine lift the edge of his quilt. Underneath was a quart of gasoline.

"I know a whole crowd," said Nine, "that needs a good switching off. "

Blake was fumbling with his keys, jamming one after another into the cell's padlock.

"There, there, don't fret." Nine was chuckling now. "I'm simply helping you along. Collective deletion! It's marvelous, don't you see?"

From his pillow he produced a match.

Death, n. A sentinel without lips.
Life, n. His impossible smile.

# SHREDS

Pierre knows that he is crumbling. After the chandelier incident, he began finding shreds of himself around the house. First came the nail slivers. Then the lashes, and finally the tears. Lately his footprints have vanished, too. This is for the best, he thinks. Grubby carpets are difficult to stitch.

# THE TAXONOMIST

Every wall in Francois' house was built of drawers. The knobs of the drawers were triangular, and ocean grey. They looked exactly like obedient flies. Inside them were naughtier insects. Neutrons. Protons. Electrons with invisible wings. Francois preferred the knobs, and the names below them. Heron. Cormorant. Finch. Names didn't bother with atoms and their trinity of chaos. That was the comfort of words. They were built of letters, and letters stood still.

Each of Francois' drawers contained a species of bird. Long ago he had plucked the skeletons clean, and arranged the bones just so. Twice an electrical storm had seared through the windows and along the walls, until the drawers retched their contents to the floor. Francois had woken to find his home transformed into a litter of white lines. Eleven months he spent sifting, knees blue, through wings, spines and skulls. A scrambled anatomy, he knew, was not impossible to cure. Within the year every bird was intact.

On the night of the second storm, Francois had fallen from his room into a version of his room. The two seemed entirely alike. Then he glanced outside. At first he saw nothing but thick brown rain. Then he noticed that the rain was not rain at all, but a flock of gulls. The gulls were tearing cylindrical holes in the sky. Soon they drew together into a triangle of flight, coasting back and forth beyond his bedroom wall. He watched the flock swell and wane like a contracting lung, until it shrank into a single, breathless gull. Francois tried to climb out of the dream, but could not unfasten his gaze from the bird. From its beak crawled dozens of flies. As Francois pried his mind awake he found that the flies were letters crawling from his own dry tongue, flooding the room with a swarm of scrambled words.

# EXPERIMENT 6: HOW TO READ

### Materials:

Page, pen, teeth.

### Procedure:

1. Fill page with words.
2. Choose one.
3. Take word in mouth.
4. Chew.
5. Swallow the seeds.
6. Spit out the shell.
7. Repeat steps 3-6 with each remaining word.
8. Notice a swelling in chest.
9. Wait.
10. Notice the first seed hatch.

To read, v. To sow.

# THE ACCIDENT

None of the townspeople knew precisely when the collision had occurred, or why. Everyone agreed that the train car had derailed, that it had clattered two kilometers before crossing Main Street and impaling the town emporium. Most agreed that the train car was full of children. No one agreed on how many, and only several citizens—young people themselves—suspected that the children were deaf.

The emporium was beyond repair. The racks had fallen, the ceiling had cracked. Towers of bread loomed between the train car and the walls, cushioning the wreckage. Cabbage fists lay shredded, and cherries rolled like candied eyes. The linoleum was blind. Provisions buried every surface, winking in the light. A miracle, said the townspeople, that light. All of the circuits intact. Only the switch was broken, leaving the bulbs frozen on.

Within the train car the children built a town of their own. They slept and ate and sorted, arranging the piles as best they could. By autumn they had amassed a small city of books. Novels, mostly. By winter, when the townspeople began to notice their naked shelves, it was too late. The children had gutted every book, stuffing the pages in their shirts for warmth. No one knew where they disposed of the binding.

In place of spoken words, the children constructed their own system of sounds. It was a musical Braille, an engine song, a whirring no adult could detect. Infants passing in prams would listen, lulled, and reach toward the shards of the emporium. The sounds transformed the shattered train into a box of speech, and seemed to restore some banished velocity. To rekindle its capacity for speed.

Mostly, the children wrote. When they'd stuffed their shirts full, they blackened whatever paper they had left. On stormy days their pages would waft into the street, plate the bicycle wheels, plaster—rain-struck—against windows. The pages were strung with definitions:

WINDOW: A membrane, often glass, whose panes rearrange themselves at night.

MOMENT: The space between
two magnets before
they collide.

MOON:   The sun's skull.

Years later, when the emporium was empty and
the houses stood mute, a band of wanderers would
arrive by the same tracks. They would live off
leaves and light, carving tools from the limbs of
sycamores. Soon the sycamores were spines,
stripped clean of bark and moss, pointing toward
something long past. The wanderers would set fire
to the trees, but not before they discovered what
the spines contained. Each was filled with the
skeletons of books.

# THE CURRENCY OF THOUGHT

Several weeks after the accident, the bureaucrats appeared. They wheeled the gramophone past the emporium, to the town square. A boy followed. As he walked, a crumpled page tumbled from his sleeve.

The boy watched the bureaucrats lift the gramophone above their heads. From its mouth came a strangled sound, then a cough. He watched one bureaucrat adjust the spindle. Another peered into the horn. When she turned back, her face was heavy with ash.

The gramophone coughed again. "Henceforth," said the mayor, "mathematics will replace speech as the national dialect."

His voice was two octaves too high. It seeped down Main Street like oil in a vein.

One of the bureaucrats noticed the fallen page. Before the boy could stop him, he was smoothing it flat against the pavement. He glanced at the words. Slowly, he tore the page in half, then in quarters. The boy watched him carry the pieces to the curb, and drop them through the slats of the gutter.

"I have banished the artists. I have banished the vowels," the mayor was saying. "Today, I banish the currency of thought."

The bureaucrat was still feeding the page into the ground. He dropped one piece, then another. He dropped some of them two at a time. When he came to the last pair, he paused. Glancing round, he let one piece fall. He slipped the other into his coat.

## HER SECOND BOOK

In December, Selma wrote a book about a town without laws. "Herd of Nouns," she called it.

It consisted entirely of verbs.

# GRAVITY

Dawn had already broken when Cornelius discovered that every object in his house was inching toward him. His coins. His wife's brooches. Dust particles tangling the light. Across the room, a dozen eggs rattled from their cardboard sleeve. They rolled forward, past the sink. Cornelius lunged in time to catch one. Eleven shattered. Still the broken shells crept on, nudging at his heels.

Cornelius stood in a pool of yolk. Dust spun round him in clots. Melinda's brooches were closer now, shredding the rug, which was bright with advancing dimes. Cornelius blinked. For the first time, he pitied the magnets in his life. In his hand the unbroken egg felt astoundingly light. Nothing to do but fry.

As Cornelius cooked the egg, he glanced outside. Next door, a man was pruning hedges. He appeared to be whistling. Cornelius tried to whistle too, and discovered that his voice had sunken to his knees. It was impossible to expel.

Cornelius flipped the egg. He waited ten seconds, then emptied the pan onto his plate. As he sat down at the table, he noticed that the coins had multiplied. They were circling his ankles in a copper blur. A brooch had climbed his shoelace and lodged itself in his sock. There it spun, painfully. Cornelius tossed it across the room only to watch it return with new ferocity. So he ate. He sipped orange juice. He read the newspaper until the letters trembled, broke free, and scuttled up his arms.

Cornelius closed his eyes. His plate was empty. His newspaper was empty. The dust was closer now, swarming his face. A few particles slipped inside his ears and began displacing his thoughts. The particles were so loud that Cornelius barely heard the word wafting from his patella. He brought his knee to his shoulder and listened. More objects were swarming him now, and the shadows of objects. The word was his name.

# EXPERIMENT 7: HOW TO BOIL

Materials:

Pot, stove, water, infant.


Procedure:

1. Lift pot onto stove.

2. Wake fire.

3. Wait.

4. Extract laugh from infant.

5. Store laugh in cool compartment, preferably in vest.

6. Deposit laugh in water.

7. Gently arrange flames beneath pot.

8. Wait.

9. Do not watch.

10. Sing lullaby as fire beams.

To boil, v. To cage laughter.

# THE PHILOSOPHER

Several days before the war, the philosopher died. The autopsy revealed a wheel in the place of his brain. He had choked on premise A of the argument for fatalism. Premise B had lodged in his ear, and premise C had coiled up his nose, into his skull. The doctors found it there, intact, knotted and double-knotted round the spokes. The wheel was moving still, driven on by inertia. In time they noticed a buzzing in his chest, and found an engine between his lungs.

"It could not have been otherwise," they murmured as they gathered their tools.

The conclusion had replaced his pulse.

## THE VIVISECTION

After Halloween, Pierre vivisected a clock. First, he extracted the slice between 12:01 and 11:59. From noon he cut off a minute, then a second, then less. The closer to the Now he came, the more time there was to cut.

Truth, n. An axis.
Knowledge, n. Its asymptote.

# THE SOLDIER

He was an old man with brown eyes and a brown beard that he knotted each morning. By noon the beard came undone, strand by strand, netting his chin and collarbones. The man didn't mind. All he minded were dirty hands. He washed them all day, until his embers cooled. The war left him swimming in embers.

The features of the man's face were extraordinarily small. His nose was the size of a thimble, his lips no wider than pins. When he washed, lenses of sweat coated his upper lip. The man liked that taste. He liked to wash until the lenses merged into a film of salt.

The man's skull would be small, too, if it weren't full of pictures. Washing kept the pictures quiet. Gently the man scrubbed the knuckles of his left hand, then his right. He was scrubbing off the edges of a picture. The picture was of a boy in a bald meadow. The sky was blank except for a popping sound. The man listened, and saw that the boy was perforated. He knelt to examine his veins. They were smooth and firm, like the boughs of a newborn tree. The boy was whispering a sentence to the ground:

"The best pleasure is the threshold of pain."

So far the man had scrubbed away the popping sound. Now he was working on the veins. Branch by branch they vanished, and then the boy vanished too. By now the man's lashes were dripping with sweat. He raised his hands, but they were raw with forgetting. His palms were two flames.

# THE WAR

# THE CELLIST

On the Saturday after the war began, Analena fell in love with her cello. One moment she was an ordinary schoolgirl, and the next she lost her capacity for speech. She played through frost and thaw, sickness and sleep. The townspeople grew so accustomed to her music that it became, for those who listened, another form of silence.

# THE WIDOW

After the war, the mayor arrived. He wore a hat strung with tassels. Crowning the hat was a stuffed bird, glass-eyed, with wings outstretched. The tassels hung from the rim of the hat, splitting his face like a sunken halo.

The townspeople followed the mayor's coach down Main Street, through the town square, past the rows of shops. They followed him to the graveyard.

One woman watched from her bedroom, between the slats of her venetian blinds. She could tell that the townspeople were empty. They looked as if they had fallen a great distance, and landed at the bottom of a well.

"We stand today," the mayor announced, "in a town of ones and zeros. The former stand, the latter sleep beneath the grass of this field." He stamped his foot so abruptly that his tassels swung. "Together we form a code of allegiance."

The woman listened. The mayor was standing inches from her husband's grave. In a moment, she thought, her husband's hands would emerge from the soil. Gently they would loop around the mayor's heels, and draw him like blood into the syringe of Earth.

# THE WIDOWER

As the mayor spoke, a man slipped from the crowd. He walked down the center of Main Street, along the split yellow lines. The shops were vacant. Pale flags dangled from the lamps.

When he reached the town emporium, the man paused. He heard something. Not a noise exactly, but a thick silence. The sound of wind. Inside, a child was standing on a stack of cereal boxes. She was winding tinsel around the ceiling pipe, where banana skins hung like chandeliers. As the man turned to go, the child looked up. They watched each other for a moment. Without smiling, the child lowered herself from the boxes, and disappeared behind a shelf. The man blinked. Again he turned, shielding his eyes against the sun. He walked until he felt a tapping on his wrist.

It was the child. She was holding a glass jar.

"Hello," said the man.

The child placed the jar in his hands. Before he could protest, she had darted back into the emporium.

The man held the jar up to his eyes. It was empty. He spun it clockwise, then counterclockwise. He unscrewed the lid and listened. Nothing. He continued walking. He walked until the shops leveled off into fields, and the fields into dust. He walked until he found a lake.

The man did not change his course. He stepped through the reeds and across the bank. The water rushed into his shoes, soaked his calves. Clouds of silt billowed at his knees. Soon the ground fell away and he was treading water, watching the horizon cleave the sun in half. He took a long breath, then emptied his lungs. As he drifted below the surface he turned the jar upside down, holding the lid in his other hand. Into the jar he whispered a single word.

Long after the war, a boy would wander off Main Street, over the fields and dust, to the same lake. He would find a jar floating among the reeds. With difficulty, he would unscrew the lid. He would listen. He would hear the echo of a word. Of a woman's name.

# EXPERIMENT 8: HOW TO FORGIVE

### Materials:

N/A

### Procedure:

1. See Experiment 4.

# FOR GOOD

From the schoolhouse, the children heard the mayor's carriage rattle off into the distance. The teacher glanced toward the windows. Dusk had switched the glass off-white.

"Is it over for good?" asked a boy.

"Is what over?" the teacher replied.

"The w—"

"We'll start with arithmetic," she interrupted, and turned to the board:

$$\text{flame} + \text{hour} =$$

"George!"

A boy stepped forward.

$$\text{flame} + \text{hour} = ash$$

"Lita," the teacher snapped, "Correct him."

A girl slipped from her chair. She took the chalk from George and solved:

flame + hour = ~~ash~~ *flames*

She looked at George. Before the teacher could speak, she wrote:

*It never ended.*

# THE WORLD

"Writing a book," said Pierre, "What's it like?"

Selma shrugged. "A world assembles."

"*A* world?"

"*A* world, *the* world, what's the difference?"

Pierre studied his wrists. "Where is it, then?"

"Where's what?"

"The world."

"Nowhere, of course."

# THE MEMORY CHAIN

Throughout his seventy years, Franz had collected 2.5 billion instants of time. He stored them in chronological order. The cross section of his mind resembled a slice of honeycomb, each hexagon brimming with seconds. The comb contained Franz's entire life, shelved away from the din of the world. Outside was a wild place, full of moments without texture or size. Each moment was safe, Franz knew, only after it occurred, once memory gave it shape. Without memory, Franz was nothing but a vacant hive.

Collecting instants was no easy task. At age four Franz had devised a system of recollection, The Memory Chain, wherein he spent each moment remembering the moment before. Every instant contained the memory of another, and so on, like the spooling of a face between two mirrors. In sleep Franz climbed down the rungs of reflection, deep into the honey of his past. He often dreamed he was a Russian doll, bloated with age, each layer the core of the next.

Some nights the layers of the doll were shells. Franz would open one piece after another, and find a Franz-shaped hollow at his core. Other nights he dreamed of an enormous centrifuge. The wheel would spin into oblivion, draining the seconds from his comb. His cells would shrink from hexagons to squares to a shapeless yellow, until his whole mind congealed into wax. I am the memory of a memory of a memory, he would think. A memory of what, he couldn't say.

# EXPERIMENT 9: HOW TO AGE

Materials:

Flute, soil.

Procedure:

1. Plant flute in soil.
2. Kneel.
3. Press lips to flute's eye.
4. Breathe once.
5. Watch soil stir.
6. Breathe twice.
7. Watch soil swell with notes.
8. Extract flute from soil.
9. Stand.
10. Plant flute in sky.

To age, v. To bury music.

# WHAT WILL HAPPEN

"Suppose I try it," said Pierre.

"Try what?" Selma blinked.

"Writing a book."

"Suppose you do."

"What will happen?"

"Words."

Pierre was gazing at the wallpaper, whose daffodils had knelt beneath a sudden wind.

"Words will happen?" he said.

"That's right. To you."

"Words will happen to me?"

"When you happen to them."

# THE MORTICIAN

Dimitri lived on the edge of town, in a cottage with ivory doors. Inside, the air was cold enough to snap. Even the quilts were brittle. One morning, a milk bottle had shattered at his touch. The opal shards were more rigid than glass.

Heat was impracticable. Dimitri's guests required temperatures of at least fifteen below. Upstairs was a room with twenty beds, the mattresses stuffed with ice. All day Dimitri watched his sleepers, admiring their faces, their pale blue hands. He'd seen most of them before, bustling through town on important errands. Their lives were a sequence of errands, he knew, each one terribly important.

Dimitri's guests seemed like ordinary citizens. They, too, had names. They had lips and noses and limbs. They were awfully polite. The only thing different about Dimitri's guests was their eyes. They were locked.

Dimitri's task was to unlock the eyes. Afterward, he sifted through memories and other fossils to recover the sleeper's last thought. Some of the thoughts were pictures, some were words. A few were unspeakably sad. Dimitri stored the thoughts in bronze vials, which he hung from the ceiling. The vials were impervious to cold.

Dimitri kept his guests for as long as he could. He winced to think of what came next. The graveyards, the disrupted flesh. Stone flowers with roots of bone. In dreams he slept beside them, lungs swollen with earth, sealed beneath the world and its rushing air. He would wake alone. In silence he would sit among the vials, bleaching the room with his breath. Now and then a thought would seep from one vial's rim, spilling down into his own, unfastened eyes.

# THE HOUSE

A man sat on the town green, eating flowers. He plucked off the leaves, then dusted his nose with the anther. After that, he started on the petals. He chewed the edges, swallowed the veins. By twilight his teeth were violet.

Windows blinked on. The sun dipped out of the sky, under the ground, and back. Still he sat. He ate one stem, then another. He hardly noticed the bureaucrat.

"You'll have to leave, sir," she said.

"Please knock," he replied.

"What's that?"

"You heard me."

"Knock on what?"

"The door."

"Where?"

"Right in front of you."

The bureaucrat ran a hand over her hair.

"If you won't knock, at least ring the bell."

"What bell?"

"Right there, on the doorframe."

"There's no bell, sir."

"Of course there is. I put it there."

The bureaucrat stepped forward.

"Careful, you'll trip!"

The bureaucrat turned. She took a few steps away, then spoke.

"You know, you can't think things into being."

"Why not?"

"I don't know. You just can't."

Slowly the man rose to his feet. He cupped his palm and twisted the air. Then he drew his arm back. In the silence, the echo of a hinge.

"If my house exists in thought," he said, "I can fashion it as I please." He smiled politely. "If I can fashion it as I please, I can fashion it real."

# THE DOLLMAKER

They were half-bloomed people, Angelica's dolls. White-eyed and ribbon-tongued, with glass teeth. From their mouths wafted a peculiar sound, not unpleasant, and almost opaque. The sound was indistinguishable from wind.

Every evening a new doll arrived. All day Angelica trimmed and stitched until a face emerged from the cloth. By dusk, ribbons streamed from the dresser drawers, and shards of fabric lay scattered on the ground. The new doll was always identical to the rest, except for the region behind its face.

Angelica filled each skull with precisely tangled yarn. Some of the brains were yellow, some were blue. Now and then an eye would come loose, and the yarn would spill through the socket. Sometimes both eyes would erupt, until all a doll could see were its woolen thoughts.

Angelica's dolls stood in lines, atop a wooden dresser. When a new doll arrived, Angelica placed it at the end of the last line, near the edge. Older dolls moved inward, displaced by the new. They were luckier than bloomed people, Angelica's dolls. Time sustained them.

Once, a doll fell. Its teeth shattered into glass so fine it resembled salt.

Angelica sent the broken doll to town. Town was nothing like the dresser. The dresser could be touched, and stood upon. Town was a collective hallucination, a fiction of the bloomed. Bloomed people were temporary, Angelica knew. For the dolls, life was neither a sequence of questions nor a gallery of pain. Life was cloth and glass and ribbons, and the sound of neighboring dolls. The world was the dresser, and the dresser's edge.

# PROGNOSES

The gramophone woke everyone at dawn.

"A town is a collection of numbers," the mayor announced. He coughed. Fists of smoke erupted from the horn. "Numbers within numbers. The time has come to make those numbers known."

The smoke was threading up the nostrils of the bureaucrats. They stood side by side beneath the gramophone, smug as moss. Their horses were stamping through the town square, chewing steel, bruising the flowers. One caught a finger of smoke, and sneezed. The spray turned the roses momentarily white. Along the road, the gardenias hung like swollen brides.

The bureaucrats were marching now. They were distributing cards to the townspeople. The townspeople's heads were hanging bells, their tongues bronze clappers. Now and then a bell would glance at her card, and produce a noise of high frequency. One of the bells clattered to the ground.

Each card contained a number. Some of the numbers were several digits long, some were two.

One of the cards contained the mouth of a bloom, of a bell: 0.

"On your cards," the mayor continued, "you will find the number of your remaining heartbeats. Even the youngest citizens will find their numbers accurate. You know by now—" He coughed again, clotting the air with ash. "That infants are nothing but new machines."

# THE NUMBER

Pierre's card read:

```



           1043401



```

He turned it over:

```



```

He brought the edge level with his eyes:

---

# THE PHOTOGRAPHER

From the branch of a nearby tree, Matilda watched the mayor speak. Before her left eye she held her time machine. She swept the lens from the mayor to the bureaucrats, from the horses to the row of open doors. Her father was standing near the end of the row. Matilda could see that he had read his card already. It had canceled something in his face.

Matilda held the lens on her father. Before she could move, she felt a whirring on her wrist. A moth. Hastily she brushed it away, only to lose her grip on the machine. It crashed through the foliage, snapping twigs to the ground. She sat immobile, both hands over her mouth. A moment passed, then two. If she looked hard enough, she might unsee the accident, reverse the fall.

To her astonishment, the lens emerged out of the green.

"Is this yours?" said a voice.

"Yes, yes it is." she said. "Who's there?"

No one answered. After a moment, Matilda shifted a branch. A tiny man was peering up at her, his nose obscured by a leaf.

"Here you are," he said, holding it up.

"You can keep it there for now," said Matilda, studying his face. "I don't want to drop it again."

"As you wish," said the man. Shyly he examined the lens, held the square of glass to his eye.

"You can take one if you'd like."

"Take what?"

"A picture."

The man reddened, smiling. "That's alright. I'll keep it safe is all, till you'd like it back."

"Don't you want to help me?"

"Help you with what?"

"With saving things."

"What sorts of things?"

"Those people over there. I'm clicking them into my machine."

"I see," said the man. He thought for a moment. "What about the other things that need saving?"

"Like what?"

"Like that branch you're sitting on. Or my hair."

Matilda gestured to the camera. "Take a picture, then."

The man blushed again. "No need."

"I can take it for you."

The man shifted his weight, then reached into his pocket. He pulled out his fist and examined it.

"Well?"

The man opened his fist. "Take this instead," he said finally, tossing something white into the branches above.

It was a card. With some difficulty, Matilda caught it. "One million, forty-three thousand, four hundred and one," she read.

They were quiet. In the distance, the gramophone was coughing plumes of ash into the emptying street.

"What did you mean," said Matilda, "about those other things that need saving?"

"Nothing you don't know already," said the man. "Just that everything's dying, all the time."

"How so?"

"This tree, for instance. No matter how healthy it is, it can't help moving closer to its end. As an acorn, it was dying. It was dying from the moment it began."

Matilda swallowed. "That's not true."

"Why not?" the man said gently. He was speaking more clearly now.

"It just isn't."

"If things lasted you wouldn't love them anymore."

Matilda said nothing.

"I'm sorry to upset you. If you'd like I can hand you your contraption, your—"

"My time machine."

"Your time machine."

"Yes."

"Why do you call it that?"

"Because it stops the moments from vanishing."

"From passing, you mean?"

Matilda nodded.

"Suppose they don't vanish."

"But they do."

"How do you know?"

"They disappear! Look," She clapped her hands and paused. "There was a moment, and now it's gone."

"So is the sun, every night."

"What?"

The man pointed at the sky, which was growing dim. "There it is, already vanishing."

"Well, not really," said Matilda with impatience. "We're turning. You know that."

The man beamed. "We're turning," he repeated. "That's just what I meant."

"About time?"

"Yes! Suppose the moments don't vanish. That they're happening still. That what's passing is you."

Matilda was watching the gramophone. Some of the bureaucrats were wincing under its weight, flipping it clockwise and back.

"You might end up there," the man was saying, his eyes bright. "In the place where every moment of your life exists at once. As it is, you're walking through the memories of a person you don't know yet—the very last version of you."

The bureaucrats had finished distributing the cards. They were heaving the gramophone onto a wagon. While they adjusted the horn, one of the horses broke free. Matilda watched it sprint down Main Street, over the fields, until it shrank to the size of a bud.

"Will you help me down?" Matilda asked.

"Of course," the man replied. He held out his hand. In his palm was a thimble.

Future, n. The memory of now.

# THE DRAFT

Pierre looks outside to find the sky descending. Helicopter blades have dismembered the clouds. Across the road, the bureaucrats are standing single file. They are sealing envelopes.

Pierre rolls the cyclist along the windowsill. Somewhere in the house, Selma's typewriter has come alive. Sentences throb from the keys.

Behind the cyclist, the helicopter lands. Pierre rolls him across the spinning blades, across the faces of the bureaucrats. The bureaucrats are marching from door to door. They are distributing envelopes.

The mayor emerges from the helicopter. His cigar is the size of a wand.

"War season," he declares. "You know what to expect. Some of you will return as ones, some as zeros."

Pierre aligns the cyclist with the mayor's face. Downstairs, the typewriter is holding its breath. Selma is finishing a novel, about a town in which no one remembers.

"You'll come to see," the mayor continues, "That zeros aren't so different from ones." He chuckles, knotting the air with smoke. "In a way, you're already zeros. You're shadows, self-thinking thoughts."

Pierre listens for the typewriter. The only sound in the house is his pulse. He assembles his needles, lifts the cyclist from the sill, and makes his way down the hallway, to the stairs.

Selma is standing below, unblinking. In her hand is an envelope.

# EXPERIMENT 10: HOW TO REMEMBER

Materials:

N/A

Procedure:

1. Do not forgive.

# THE WHITE BALLOON, PART II

How the world ended, according to Pierre:

## I

In the end, the Child took her hourglass
and began to climb: trees, homes, steeples.
No object brought her high enough.

## II

She strapped rockets to her knees
and plunged down in smoke.

## III

She bound the legs of a dozen birds
with thread, closed her eyes, felt them carry her up,
above the chimneys, parallel to the clouds,
but they tangled with the wind
and drifted back.

## IV

The white balloon, and the word inside,
were always just beyond her reach.

## V

So the Child summoned rain.
She scrambled up from drop to drop
but each fell faster than she could climb.

## VI

She caught a lightning branch in her fist
and held on as it pulled her back into the sky,
above the storm, higher than she had ever been.

## VII

And in the blue bright air
the Child saw that the white balloon
was even farther away than she had thought.

## VIII

In her wonder, the Child
let the hourglass slip from her hands.

## IX

It never stopped falling.
And the Child never stopped reaching
toward the word she once knew.

# HIS AUTOBIOGRAPHY, REVISED

<u>Pierre</u>

*January:* [unwritten]

*February:* [unwritten]

*March:* [unwritten]

*April:* [unwritten]

*May:* [unwritten]

*June:* [unwritten]

*July:* [unwritten]

*August:* [unwritten]

*September:* [unwritten]

*October:* [unwritten]

*November:* [*]

*December:* [unwritten]

*Pierre has been mending since noon, when he woke without a shadow. Now he is finished searching. There is one more rip to sew. He steps across the carpet to the lavatory. Downstairs, the kettle is whistling with Selma's tea water. On the way Pierre glances in the mirror, and sees only daffodils.

Lindsay Stern grew up in New York City. She lives in Massachusetts, where she is completing her B.A. in English and Philosophy at Amherst College. This is her first book.

www.thescrambler.com